THIS WALKER BOOK BELONGS TO:

_____

_____

_____

_____

First published 1987 by
Walker Books Ltd
87 Vauxhall Walk
London SE11 5HJ

This edition published 2005 for Index Books Ltd

2 4 6 8 10 9 7 5 3

© 1987 Colin West

This book has been typeset in Optima

Printed in China

British Library Cataloguing in Publication Data:
a catalogue record for this book is
available from the British Library

ISBN 0-7445-8256-3

www.walkerbooks.co.uk

"Not me," said the Monkey

Colin West

WALKER BOOKS
AND SUBSIDIARIES

LONDON • BOSTON • SYDNEY • AUCKLAND

"Who keeps dropping banana skins round here?" growled the lion.

"Not me," said the monkey.

"Who keeps walking all over me?" hissed the snake.

"Not me," growled the lion.
"And not me," said the monkey.

"Who keeps throwing coconuts about?" snorted the rhino.

"Not me," hissed
    the snake.
"Not me," growled
    the lion.
"And not me,"
    said the monkey.

"WHO KEEPS TICKLING ME?"
roared the elephant.

"Not me," snorted the rhino.
"Not me," hissed the snake.
"Not me," growled the lion.

"And not ME!"
said the monkey.

Slurp! Slurp! Slurp!
went the elephant.

WHOOOOOSH!

"Now who's going to stop
all this monkey business?"
laughed the lion, and the snake,
and the rhino, and the elephant.

"Well..."

"NOT ME!"
said You-Know-Who.

COLIN WEST says everyone loves monkeys and chimps, "probably because they remind us of ourselves so much!" In **"Not me," said the monkey** he was keen to create a cheeky character that actually had the last laugh. Colin says, "Maybe *you've* been called a 'cheeky monkey' before – but I hope not too often! By the way, did you notice that the front endpapers are different to those at the end?"

Colin West enjoys working on all types of book, including poetry and story books. He is the author/illustrator of many books, including the Giggle Club titles *Buzz, Buzz, Buzz, Went Bumble-bee*; *"I Don't Care!" Said the Bear*; *One Day in the Jungle* and *"Only Joking!" Laughed the Lobster* as well as the jungle tales *"Go tell it to the toucan!"*; *"Have you seen the crocodile?"*; *"Hello, great big bullfrog!"* and *"Pardon?" said the giraffe*. Colin lives in Epping, Essex.